Survive

Survive

Anna-Stina Johansson

Rebecca was about to put away the mop in the closet in the supply room when a man jumped out from the shadow behind the door. She wanted to scream but the sharp knife on her throat silenced her.

"Shut up bitch! Make one noise and I'll kill ya." His eyes glared with contempt.

The cold concrete wall scraped against her back as he pressed her against it. "Please don't kill me!" She put her hand in her pocket. "Here, I just got my pay check."

"I don't want your damn money! And I told you to shut up!" He gave her a shrewd look and leaned forward. "All I want is you." His bad breath made her want to gag. He punched her in the tummy. Rebecca fell and gasped for air but he was already on top of her, yanking off her belt to tie her arms with it.

One look at his nasty grin made her realize that she wasn't going to escape. He was like a giant compared to her. Her tears almost blinded her. "Please don't kill me!"

He gave her a scornful smile. "I guess you have to wait and see if I make your wish come true or not." The knife gleamed from the sunlight that had seeped in through the small window. He threw his head back and laughed so hard that spit landed on her face.

Rebecca recognized the laughter. She had recently heard it but couldn't remember where. But wait, it must have been when she cleaned the corridor outside the construction workers' canteen. Even then his raw laughter had sent chills down her spine and she had hurried to wipe the floor. He had got all quiet again and was looking down at her breasts. His eyes got bigger and it looked like he was ready to eat her alive. He tore apart her blouse, grabbed one of her breasts and saliva started dripping down his chin.

The pain from his brutal touch spread throughout her body. "Please don't kill me," she said over and over again.

"Damn you! I told you to shut the hell up!" He looked at his watch and his eyes got darker.

"Damn, my break is almost over!" He looked around, found a cloth on the floor and gagged her with it. Then he abruptly turned her over so her nose hit the floor. It started bleeding. He didn't care as he pulled down her pants.

Rebecca embraced the coldness from the floor because the cold numbed the pain. The tears kept coming in a never ending stream and together with the blood it formed a puddle. She screamed silently every time he pushed himself into her. He stopped for a moment and let his fingers slide through her long hair. "I love it!" Then he started pushing himself into her again, again and again, finally he withdrew himself from her and laid down puffing besides her. "You see, I'm a nice fellow, I'll let you live considering you won't tell anyone about this." Then he caressed her throat with the knife. She closed her eyes, thinking that this was it, that her life would end now. "You sure don't look so snobbish now like you did yesterday because then you didn't even bother to turn around when I whistled at you. It feels good to have put you in your place," he grinned. "Maybe we should do it all over again sometime soon." By now he was laughing and then he left her bleeding on the floor.

Her arms were still tied behind her back but yet she managed to pull up her pants. Thereafter she pulled up her legs and put her arms around them, but she wasn't able to open up the belt. She could tell that she was bleeding between her legs. She was unable to stand up. What will she do if he came back? Rebecca tried to rise once more but her legs buckled. She crept behind the shelf full with hospital linen and curled up in fetal position. She shivered, tried to cover herself as well as she could with her ripped blouse. The sun had vanished. She looked up and managed to see a little bit of the cloudy sky. Rain had started to fall. Eventually the raindrops poured down like the tears on her cheeks. She lost track of time. Something in her had died. It was like the world didn't exist anymore. She was the only one left. A sharp pain from her diaphragm spread through her body. The nosebleed had stopped but her blocked nose made it hard to breathe. Disgust, fear, and shame spun round and round in her head. One thought that kept popping up was the thought of dying. *God, take me home, I don't want to live any more.* Her sobbing faded away. Her eyelids got heavy and she drowsed off of pure exhaustion.

A couple of hours later she woke up all disoriented. She thought she heard a dog scratching on the half-open window and

someone calling. Rebecca looked up but

couldn't see anyone. She must have

imagined it. For one short moment she had

forgotten about what had happened.

However, she only had to stretch out her

legs to remember. The pain made her start

crying again. Suddenly she heard a dog bark

and someone knocking on the door. Her

heart pounded when she heard a man's

voice!

"I'm a police officer. Are you alright, Miss?"

She didn't dare to breathe. What did he

say? Was he a police man? Maybe she could

trust him, but what if it was someone just

claiming to be a police officer? After all it's a

man's voice. Perhaps he goes away if I'm

quiet.

"Are you okay?"

She squeezed her eyes closed, numb with
terror.

"I will open the door now. Don't be afraid.
I'm here to help you."

Rebecca froze when she heard the door

open. Her heart stopped and she tried to

make herself as tiny she could there behind

the shelf. Then she felt someone pushing gently on her back. She turned her head and was greeted by big brown eyes and a lick on her face. That was the most beautiful German Shepard she'd ever seen! She couldn't help but smile. He lay down next to her. "Hi there big fellow!" She stroked him on the side. Then he rolled on his back. "Oh, you want me to scratch your tummy?" He barked and kept looking at her with his begging eyes. Her smile got bigger as she started scratching his tummy.

"His name is Amigo."

She stiffened when she heard the voice

again. She had forgotten about the man.

She hadn't even noticed that he had come

closer. He stood next to the window now.

"I'm not going to hurt you." He took off his hat.

That old fashioned gesture made her more comfortable with his presence.

"Amigo is my partner; we've worked

together for years. He's my right hand."

Amigo barked again. She started to caress

Amigo's head but she didn't look up. The

police officer sat down on the floor.

"I'm Luis. And you?" He gave her a friendly smile.

"Rebecca." Her voice came out as a whisper. He was looking at her, his eyes narrowed. She looked down, realized that her torn blouse was spotted with blood and the crotch of her pants was dark with it.

"Do you have any pets?" His voice sounded funny, choked.

First she nodded, than shook her head. "I mean no, I had a dog but he died a month ago.

"I'm so sorry to hear that. What did he die of?"

Rebecca tried desperately to cover herself with the ripped blouse, but it showed more than it covered. She fingered the garment. "Well, he was 13 years old..." Her voice faded away.

"I see." Luis took off his jacket and put it carefully around her. Then he gently untied her arms. She shivered at his touch and started to tremble. "Don't worry, I won't hurt you." He stepped back.

Amigo stretched out his legs. Rose. Sat down again, placing his body close to

Rebecca and demanded a hug from her. She couldn't resist him. Amigo put his head on her shoulder and sighed, which made her smile. Luis smiled too and let them sit like that for a while before he broke the silence. "Will you please let me take you to a doctor?"

She looked up briefly. When their eyes met it felt like she could trust him. She couldn't put the finger on why; she just knew that he wasn't going to hurt her. "I'm afraid I can't do that." She was still hugging Amigo.

"But Amigo and I will follow you."

"I don't think you understood me right."

He smiled again at her. "Then make me understand."

"I meant that I don't think that I have the strength to go see one. Last time I tried to stand I fell."

"If you let me, I can carry you."

She stopped hugging Amigo and looked straight into Luis' eyes. Was he crazy or what? She was bleeding couldn't he see that? "Carry me?"

"Yes." He had a catching smile. "Don't you think I'm strong enough to do that?" He bent his arm to show her his muscles.

She smiled. What a silly man this was.

"Well, I don't doubt that but I thought of that I'm not clean..." Once again her voice faded away.

"In my eyes you're perfect." He gave her a warm smile.

What a weird man this was. He was so kind. Maybe she should let him help her. "Okay."

"Good!" He walked towards her. Bent down and put her arms around his neck. Then he placed one arm under her knees and the

other behind her back, and then he gently

lifted her up.

Amigo strutted in front of them like he was
leading the way.

*

When she came out from the

examination room she fell down on her

knees and hugged Amigo. She cried and

then Amigo licked away her tears which

made her giggle. Luis got moved by

watching them. "I can let him stay with you

for a while if you want to, to protect you?"

Her face lit up. "I would love that!" Then she got serious. "But I can't walk him yet..."

"Don't worry about that." Luis gave her his easy smile. "I'll come by and do that if that's okay with you?"

"Yes."

And those were the last words she spoke to another person for a very long time. She didn't leave her cottage. It was Amigo who listened to her story over and over again. When she woke up screaming from a nightmare Amigo was there for her. He jumped up to her bed and let her hug him for as long as she wanted. Her tears wet his fur. He stayed with her until the sobbing faded away and she had fallen asleep again.

A few weeks went by and eventually she didn't have any tears left. Rebecca knew that she would never have survived if it hadn't been for Amigo. He gave her routines to follow since she had to open the door for his master three times a day. The first days she didn't say one word to Luis, she didn't even dare to look into his eyes. Rebecca thought that he was weird because he didn't take any notice of that, he just chatted on, talking about the weather.

As time went by she started talking to Luis. Nothing important, just about what she wanted him to buy, because it was he who brought groceries to her. Eventually, she started to follow them out on their walks and she enjoyed feeling the sun on her face again. Where she walked along the road with Luis and Amigo she felt an inner peace that she hadn't felt since before that day two months ago.

"Would you like to have some tea with me tomorrow evening?" She regretted right away what she'd said when they had reached her cottage. She wasn't ready for that!

"Yes, I would love that," he smiled, his eyes full of warm light.

She tried to smile back. She shouldn't have asked!

"Are you wondering about something?"

"No." She answered so fast that he probably understood that she lied.

"I'll be happy to listen."

"There's nothing to talk about. I'll see you tomorrow." She gave him a strained smile and then she shut the door behind him.

*

The following evening the doorbell rang. She jumped. What had she been thinking? She liked him since he made her smile. She opened up the safety chain. But why on earth had she invited him? No matter how kind he was, after all he was a man. The doorbell rang again. She unlocked the door. As he entered he gave her a bouquet of flowers. She smiled. "Thanks!"

"You're welcome!" He winked at her and reached out his hand to touch her hair. "I love your hair!"

She dropped the flowers on the floor, ran into the bedroom and locked the door. Rebecca sat down on the floor and started swaying back and forth. She shouldn't have invited him. She reached for the scissors.

Luis knocked on the door. "Are you alright?"

She didn't answer. "If you don't want to talk to me at least talk to Amigo, please."

Now she heard Amigo scratching on the door.

"Please let us in, I won't hurt you."

She rose but hesitated.

"I'm sorry that I made you upset. I just want to know that everything is okay with you." She owed them that much. She opened the door holding the scissors in her hand.

Amigo nudged her on the legs. She sat down and hugged him. Luis joined them and removed the scissors from her hand.

"What were you going to do with this?"

"Cut off my hair."

"Why?"

"He said he liked my long hair." She looked straight into his eyes.

"I'm sorry, I didn't know." His eyes were dark with sympathy.

He squeezed her hands. "Don't change the

way you look because of him. You should

only do that if you want to," he paused,

smiled gently. "However, your hairdo

doesn't matter to me because I'm crazy

about you!"

Rebecca giggled. He put her arm around her

and amazingly...it didn't frighten her. She

sighed. "Thanks for being my hero." Then

she kissed him on the cheek. His eyes got

teary.

She buried her face in his chest and drifted off in his arms with Amigo lying next to their feet.